A TEMPLAR BOOK

This book is based on the episode *The Shortest Day* from the TV series Gigantosaurus™.
Screenplay by Franck Salomé, Nicholas Sedel and Fernando Worcel.
The TV series Gigantosaurus™ is created and produced by Cyber Group Studios.
Based on the original characters created by Jonny Duddle in the book
Gigantosaurus, first published by Templar Books in 2014.

First published in the UK in 2020 by Templar Books,
an imprint of Bonnier Books UK,
4th Floor, Victoria House
Bloomsbury Square, London WC1B 4DA
Owned by Bonnier Books
Sveavägen 56, Stockholm, Sweden
www.bonnierbooks.co.uk

ISBN 978-1-78741-819-6

Adapted by Mandy Archer
Edited by Samuel Fern and Katie Haworth
Designed by Kate Wakeham
Additional design by Adam Allori
Production controller: Ché Creasey

Printed in Poland

MIX
Paper from
responsible sources
FSC
www.fsc.org   FSC® C018236

GIGANTOSAURUS™

THE BEST DAY EVER

templar
books

It was early morning in Cretacia. Tiny stretched out her arms and smiled at the sunrise. The little dinosaur hurried to find her friends. She wondered what exciting things they would do today.

"I can't wait to get started!"

It's going to be another SUN-SATIONAL day!

But Bill, Mazu and Rocky weren't excited in the slightest.

"Isn't today the SHORTEST day of the year?" yawned Bill.

"Yes," grumbled Mazu. "It's the day the sun sets the earliest."

Rocky gave his ball a grumpy kick. There wasn't enough time to have any fun.

Tiny caught the ball on her head, but her friends didn't even smile.

"What if I found a way to make the shortest day just as fun as every other day?" she suggested.

Mazu wasn't sure. "How can it be just as fun when it's shorter?"

We can have a party! And keep it going after sunset!

"But you'd need lights," sighed Mazu.

"And food," chipped in Bill. "LOTS of food."

"Yes!" nodded Tiny, "all kinds of stuff! I'll invite everybody!"

It was settled. Tiny was having a shortest-day party! The delighted triceratops skipped around Cretacia, giving out invitations to everyone she saw.

Along the way, she sang a little song:

Please come to my party, my shortest-day party. You'll see that this day is the FUNNEST OF FUN!

Tiny sang on and on. She described yummy food, music, games and magical decorations – plus presents for everyone!

Please come to my party,
my shortest-day party.
I'll show you this day
is the BEST of the year.

Tiny's friends gathered around. At first they
were cross at being disturbed, but the plans sounded
so SPECTACULAR, they started to get excited.
Everyone agreed to come!

STOMP! STOMP! STOMP! The ground shook . . . and GIGANTO appeared!

Tiny gulped nervously, then stepped forward so the huge dinosaur could see her.

W-w-would YOU like to come to my party?

"ROOOARRR!" said Giganto, then disappeared back into the jungle.

"I'll mark you down as a 'maybe'!" Tiny said, hopefully.

Tiny worked hard all day, preparing for the shortest-day party. She'd decided to have it up in the Frozen Lands, so she packed everything onto her sleigh, and Bill, Mazu and Rocky hitched a ride through the snow.

YIPPEE!

Tiny whooshed across the ice, pulling her friends behind her. At last the sleigh skidded to a stop in front of a big, green tree.

BUMP! All of Tiny's packing tumbled onto the snow – there were boxes and parcels everywhere.

"Too late!" shouted Mazu. "Look!"

Tiny gazed across the snowy mountains. Her guests were nearly here!

"Oh no," she gasped. "I spent so long telling everyone about the party, I didn't leave any time to set it up!"

She didn't know what to do.

Tiny's friends couldn't wait for the fun to begin.

"Welcome to my shortest-day party!" said Tiny, hurriedly unpacking everything.

The little dino did her best, but nothing went the way she had planned.

Where are those games you promised?

"Oh right," stammered Tiny, grabbing some garlands. "Decorations!"

She tossed the garlands up onto the tree, but they tangled messily in the branches.

"Umm . . . interesting choice . . ." said Archie.

"Where's all the food?" demanded Rugo the rat.

"Right here, as promised," said Tiny. "Have some fruit!"

Rugo swallowed the berry in one gulp, then shrieked in surprise. It was ice-cold!

Tiny shrugged uneasily. "I guess that's why they call it the 'Frozen Lands'."

BRAIN FREEZE!

"And where's the tunes?" said Ignatius. "You said there would be music."

"I've got lots of instruments in here," replied Tiny. She threw a huge trumpet over to him, but Ignatius could barely hold it, let alone play!

The poor dino fell backwards into the snow.

Tiny's shortest-day party was turning into a DISASTER. Totor and Cror decided to go home.

"Boring games, frozen food and bad music," snapped Totor.

Do you call this fun?

We call this LAME!

More guests began to grumble. One by one, they trudged away.

"Don't leave!" begged Tiny. "We're only getting started! I have presents for everyone!"

She staggered across the snow carrying the most ENORMOUS pile of gifts wrapped up in bright colours.

But the pile began to wobble, and Tiny stumbled in the snow. OH NO! The parcels tumbled down the frozen mountain, falling into a deep hole at the bottom.

Rocky, Bill and Mazu ran to their friend.

"Tiny!" gasped Rocky. "Are you all right?"

Tiny burst into tears. All she wanted was to show everyone that even the shortest day of the year could be the best!

"Maybe you're right," she sobbed. "Maybe today is just NO FUN at all."

My party . . .
it's RUINED!

Tiny's friends knew how hard she was trying. But before they could help her, a terrible roar shook the mountains. One more guest was on his way . . .

GIGANTOSAURUS!

The other dinosaurs were furious.

"What's HE doing here?" they demanded.

"I invited him . . ." Tiny said. "He deserves to have fun too."

Tiny stepped out to greet the big, scary dinosaur.

"I'm sorry I invited you out here," she said sadly. "I know I promised you lots of food and presents."

Giganto glared down at the frightened party guests. Then he thumped his tail hard against the ice. The ground began to shake.

I'm so sorry. Please don't be angry!

BOOM! BOOM! BOOM!

Tiny and her friends found themselves being bounced up and down.

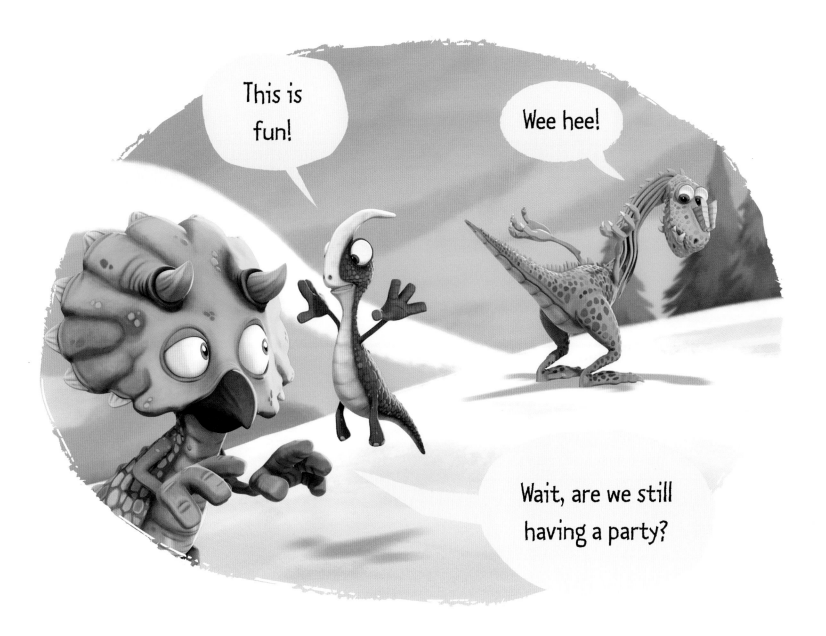

Giganto was trying to PLAY with them! Dinosaurs went sliding around in circles and icicles jingled merrily in the tree.

Tiny was confused. The party was in full swing even without food, decorations and presents.

"All those things you came for," she said. "They never happened!"

But Tiny's friends hadn't come for the promises . . .

We came to be with YOU!

That's when Tiny knew that her shortest-day party was going to be okay after all.

"Thanks, you guys. It's not the treats that make a party, it's the friends!" she cried. "Right, Giganto?"

Giganto replied with another careful tail thud, lifting the decorations on the tree and undoing all the tangles.

Now the tree was perfect.

But Giganto wasn't quite finished. He hit the ground again, even harder, shaking the mountain so much the lost presents bounced up out of the hole.

"Thank you, Giganto!" gasped Tiny, running to collect them.

What a party it turned out to be! When night fell, Cretacia turned into a winter wonderland.

Tiny took out a gigantic walnut, carefully wrapped in leaves, and presented it to Giganto.

"This is for you," she smiled. "Happy shortest day!"

ROAARRR! He had enjoyed the shortest-day party too!

Everyone cheered. "BEST DAY EVER!"

"Thanks, guys," said Tiny. "We should celebrate like this every year!"